S0-ABD-641

The Cat that Went
WOOF!

A humorous story
in a familiar setting

This edition first published in 2009
by Sea-to-Sea Publications
Distributed by Black Rabbit Books
P.O. Box 3263
Mankato, Minnesota 56002

Text © Martyn Beardsley 2004, 2009
Illustration © Lisa Smith 2004

Printed in China

All rights reserved

A CIP catalog record for this book is
available from the Library of Congress.

ISBN 978-1-59771-166-1

9 8 7 6 5 4 3 2 1

Published by arrangement with the
Watts Publishing Group Ltd, London.

Series Editor: Jackie Hamley
Series Advisors: Dr. Linda Gambrell,
Dr. Barrie Wade, Dr. Hilary Minns
Series Designer: Peter Scoulding

The Cat that Went
WOOF!

Written by
Martyn Beardsley

Illustrated by
Lisa Smith

SEA-TO-SEA
Mankato Collingwood London

Martyn Beardsley

"I love writing and reading stories. I like spooky stories best. I also like soccer and other sports. I hope you enjoy the book!"

Lisa Smith

"I love to draw. I have been drawing all my life. I like to draw animals best. I hope you will have fun with Jack, Tiger, and Patch."

Tiger lived with Jack.

They were the best of friends.

Then along came Patch.
Everything changed.

Everyone laughed when
Patch barked.

They patted his head when he
wagged his tail.

So Tiger decided she would learn to bark.

Then everyone would laugh and pat her head!

"WOOF!" said Tiger.

"Mom, I think Tiger's got a cough!" said Jack.

"WOOF! WOOF!" said Tiger
when the mail arrived.

"Mom, I think Tiger's swallowed a letter!" said Jack.

19

They took Tiger to see the vet.
"What's wrong?" asked the vet.

"She doesn't sound very well," said Jack.

"WOOF!" said Tiger.

"I see!" said the vet.

23

"Do you have any other pets?"
asked the vet.

"A new puppy called Patch!"
said Jack.

"*I see!*" said the vet.

"Then plenty of love and stroking
should solve the problem!"
said the vet.

"MIAOW!" said Tiger.
"MIOOF!" said Patch.

Notes for parents and teachers

READING CORNER has been structured to provide maximum support for new readers. The stories may be used by adults for sharing with young children. Primarily, however, the stories are designed for newly independent readers, whether they are reading these books in bed at night, or in the reading corner at school or in the library.

Starting to read alone can be a daunting prospect. **READING CORNER** helps by providing visual support and repeating words and phrases, while making reading enjoyable. These books will develop confidence in the new reader, and encourage a love of reading that will last a lifetime!

If you are reading this book with a child, here are a few tips:

1. Make reading fun! Choose a time to read when you and the child are relaxed and have time to share the story.

2. Encourage children to reread the story, and to retell the story in their own words, using the illustrations to remind them what has happened.

3. Give praise! Remember that small mistakes need not always be corrected.

READING CORNER covers three grades of early reading ability, with three levels at each grade. Each level has a certain number of words per story, indicated by the number of bars on the spine of the book, to allow you to choose the right book for a young reader:

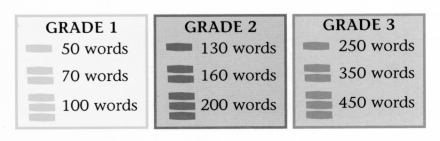

GRADE 1	GRADE 2	GRADE 3
50 words	130 words	250 words
70 words	160 words	350 words
100 words	200 words	450 words

37098101196955
READER BEAR
BEARDSLEY, MARTYN
THE CAT THAT WENT WOOF
7/09 g

PENNSAUKEN FREE PUBLIC LIBRARY
5605 CRESCENT BLVD.
PENNSAUKEN, NJ 08110